AR PTS
0.5
AR RL
4.5

D1762998

MARTINA HINGIS

BY RICHARD RAMBECK

248 LIBRARY
SUTTON ELEMENTARY SCHOOL

(Photo on front cover)
Martina Hingis returns a shot from Russia's Anna Kournikova during their women's singles semifinal match on the Center Court at Wimbledon. Thursday July 3, 1997.

(Photo on previous pages)
Martina Hingis reacts after defeating Venus Williams during the women's singles finals match at the U.S. Open. September 7, 1997.

GRAPHIC DESIGN
Robert A. Honey, Seattle

PHOTO RESEARCH
James R. Rothaus, James R. Rothaus & Associates

ELECTRONIC PRE-PRESS PRODUCTION
Robert E. Bonaker, Graphic Design & Consulting Co.

PHOTOGRAPHY
All photos by Associated Press AP

Text copyright © 1999 by The Child's World®, Inc.
All rights reserved. No part of this book may be reproduced or utilized in any form or by any means without written permission from the publisher.
Printed in the United States of America.

Library of Congress Cataloging-in-Publication Data
Rambeck, Richard
Martina Hingis / by Richard Rambeck
p. cm.
Summary: A brief look at the tennis career of the young woman who won three of the four Grand Slam tournaments in 1997.
ISBN 1-56766-519-5 (library : reinforced : alk. paper)

1. Hingis, Martina, 1980- — Juvenile literature.
2. Women tennis players—Slovakia—Biography—Juvenile literature.
[1. Hingis, Martina. 2. Women tennis players. 3. Tennis players. 4. Women—Biography] I. Title
GV994.h56r36 1998
796.342'092 — dc21
[B]

97-44094
CIP
AC

CONTENTS

7
GRAF RATES HINGIS

7
YOUNGEST TOP RANKED

8
THREE GRAND SLAMS

8
PLAYING HURT

11
HINGIS LOSES TO MAJOLI

12
MARTINA'S NAMESAKE

12
JUNIOR GRAND SLAM

15
U.S. OPEN

16
FIVE IN A ROW

16
TOP SEED IN THE U.S.

19
HINGIS VS DAVENPORT

20
BEST IN THE WORLD

20
TURNS SEVENTEEN

23
BEST TO COME

Unseeded Martina Hingis of Switzerland returns a shot against the world's No. 7 player Gabriela Sabatini of Argentina during the Toray Pan Pacific Open tennis tournament in Tokyo, Japan. January 30, 1996.

GRAF RATES HINGIS

Steffi Graf could see it. She could see what a good tennis player Martina Hingis was going to be. Graf, the top–ranked player in the world at the beginning of 1997, knew the 16–year–old Hingis was improving every day. After she lost to Graf in the semifinals of the 1996 U.S. Open, Hingis won two tournament titles in the last few months of 1996. "She's had an incredible year," Graf said. "Especially in the last few months, she seemed not afraid of playing the top players."

YOUNGEST TOP RANKED

No, Hingis wasn't afraid of playing anybody, including Graf. "She's definitely one of the few players who will always make life difficult," Graf said. Hingis did more than just make life difficult. She took over Graf's top ranking in the world in March of 1997. Only 16, Hingis was the youngest female ever to be ranked as the world's top player. Hingis didn't lose a match in the first five months of 1997. She won the Australian Open in January, her first title in a Grand Slam event.

THREE GRAND SLAMS

In fact, Hingis almost won all four Grand Slam tournaments in 1997. (There are four tournaments in the Grand Slam: the Australian Open, the French Open, Wimbledon, and the U.S. Open.) Hingis might have won the Grand Slam if it hadn't been for a horse. Several weeks before the French Open, Hingis was doing one of her favorite things, horseback riding. Unfortunately, she fell off the horse and injured her knee. She had to have surgery on the knee and missed three tournaments as a result.

PLAYING HURT

Hingis actually was worried that she wouldn't be healthy enough to play in the French Open. After taking some time off, she was able to practice before the French Open. "I just can't wait to start

Hingis in action during her quarter-final match against Irina Spirlea of Romania at the Australian Open Tennis Championship in Melbourne, Australia. January 22, 1997.

Hingis reacts after defeating Monica Seles of the USA 6–7, 7–5, 6–4 in the semifinals of the French Open tennis tournament in Paris, France. June 5, 1997.

playing again," Hingis said. "I was starting to miss tennis." Although her knee hurt, Hingis was able to make it to the finals, where she faced 19-year-old Iva Majoli. For the first time in 1997, Hingis didn't win a match. Majoli was just a little bit better than Hingis. "I played the match of my life," Majoli said. "I didn't give her a chance to play her game."

HINGIS LOSES TO MAJOLI

Hingis didn't blame the loss on her knee injury, even though it was clear that she wasn't fully healthy. "This was the best match I've seen her play," Hingis said of Majoli. "I got a little tired in the end, but it wasn't just because I was injured." Hingis didn't take the loss too hard. After all, it was only the second time she had ever been in the finals of a Grand Slam tournament. Yes, she was the top-ranked player in the world, but she was also only 16. She had been a pro for less than three years.

MARTINA'S NAMESAKE

Martina Hingis seemed destined to be a great tennis player. She was named after one of the greatest players ever, Martina Navratilova. In addition, Hingis's mother, Melanie Molitor was a former tennis champion herself. Hingis was born on September 30, 1980, in Kosice, Slovakia. She started playing tennis at age 3 and entered her first tournament when she was 5. When Martina was 7, she and her mother moved to Switzerland, where Hingis still lives. (Melanie Molitor is divorced from Martina's father, Karol Hingis.)

Top-seeded Hingis prepares to serve to Anna Kournikova of Russia in the third round of the French Open tennis tournament, May 31, 1997. Hingis won 6–1, 6–3.

JUNIOR GRAND SLAM

In 1993, at age 12, Hingis entered the Junior French Open. She won, becoming the youngest girl ever to win a Junior Grand Slam tournament. One year later, 13–year–old Martina was ranked as the 399th best female player in the world. Hingis turned pro in October of 1994. Naturally, she won her first tournament

Framed by a rainbow, Hingis of Switzerland holds up her women's singles trophy outside the Arther Ashe Stadium at the U.S. Open in New York, September 7, 1997. Hingis defeated Venus Williams of Palm Beach Gardens, Florida in straight sets 6–0, 6–4.

as a professional. In June of 1995, Hingis was ranked in the top 20 in the world. She was still only 14 years old. Less than a month before her 15th birthday, Hingis made it all the way to the semifinals of the 1995 U.S. Open.

U.S. OPEN

Martina Hingis didn't win that 1995 Open. Steffi Graf did. Hingis didn't win the 1996 U.S. Open, either. Graf won it again. But there would be a new champion in 1997. After losing the final of the 1997 French Open, Hingis prepared to play in the tournament she had always dreamed of winning: Wimbledon. Her knee was feeling fine. Unfortunately for Graf, her own knee was badly injured, and she would not be able to defend her Wimbledon title. Hingis roared into the finals without losing a set.

FIVE IN A ROW

In the finals, Hingis faced Jana Novotna. The older, more experienced Novotna gave Hingis a lesson in the first set, winning 6–2. Hingis bounced back to take the second set 6–3, but fell behind 2–0 in the third set. Novotna was one point away from a 3–0 lead in that set, but she hit an easy return into the net. Suddenly, Hingis became unbeatable. She won five games in a row and wound up winning the set 6–3. Martina Hingis won the 1997 Wimbledon championship. "I knew I wasn't in great shape at the French Open, but this time I knew I could do it," Hingis said.

Wimbledon Women's Singles champion Hingis holds her trophy, July 6, 1997. Hingis defeated Jana Novotna 2–6, 6–3, 6–3, in the final, to become the youngest winner of the championship this century.

TOP SEED IN THE U.S.

Novotna was quite impressed with Hingis. "Even though Martina is very young, I have a lot of respect for her," Novotna said. "She is very professional, she is very talented and very respectful of the other players. She's also a nice person who enjoys her success." Less

Hingis smiles as she looks at her mother sitting in the stands after losing the first set to Lindsey Davenport during their semifinals match in the Acura Classic tennis tournament, August 9, 1997.

than two months later, Hingis was the youngest female ever to be the top seed in the U.S. Open. Graf was still unable to play because of her knee injury. As a result, Hingis was expected to win easily. She did exactly what she was expected to do.

HINGIS VS DAVENPORT

Hingis reached the semifinals without losing a set. In the semis, she faced Lindsay Davenport, who had defeated Hingis earlier in the year in a tournament in Los Angeles. The loss to Davenport was only the second of the year for Hingis. (The other was in the French Open finals.) In the U.S. Open, Hingis beat Davenport easily, 6–2, 6–4. "She's playing really well," Davenport said. "She's going to be pretty tough to beat." Hingis proved that in the finals. Facing U.S. star Venus Williams, Hingis won 6–0, 6–4.

BEST IN THE WORLD

Hingis had won three of the four Grand Slam tournaments in 1997. Only the loss in the French Open final to Iva Majoli kept her from winning the Grand Slam. "You always want to win the Grand Slam tournaments," Hingis said. "It doesn't matter what year or what time you win them." Hingis was, without a doubt, the best player in the world. "It's kind of fun, seeing the attention is on you," she said. "Everyone is expecting you to have a great tournament. I like the attention."

TURNS SEVENTEEN

Hingis didn't turn 17 until three weeks after winning the 1997 U.S. Open. She was still young, but she also was clearly the brightest star on the women's tour. "She's special because she's mature beyond her years," said Pam Shriver, a former top player. "She has great court sense. She knows how to play the points well." Mary Joe Fernandez, a current star, believes Hingis is practically

Hingis raises the trophy after defeating Venus Williams in the women's singles finals match at the U.S. Open, September 7, 1997. Hingis defeated Williams 6–0, 6–4.

Hingis hugs the Australian Open trophy after she won the final against Conchita Martinez of Spain, in Melbourne, Australia, January 31, 1998. Hingis won the final 6–3, 6–3.

impossible to defeat. "When she's playing well, Fernandez said, "you have to play almost perfect tennis to beat her."

BEST TO COME

The amazing thing is, Hingis still has most of her best days ahead. "Maybe tomorrow I will realize I won this tournament," Hingis said. "It feels great, like a dream come true. Everyone is expecting me to beat every player in the world right now," Hingis said of being ranked No. 1. "But if I don't make it, it doesn't matter. In tennis you have so many chances. When you don't play well in one tournament, the next week there's another one."